Nikki Giovanni:
A Special Poet

by Jacqueline Churchill
illustrated by Jamie Smith

 HOUGHTON MIFFLIN   BOSTON

Nikki Giovanni is a famous poet. Her poems are read by children and adults all over the world. But why did Nikki begin writing poetry? And how did she decide what to write about?

Nikki was born in Knoxville, Tennessee, on June 7, 1943. When she was a little girl, she and her family moved near Cincinnati, Ohio. Nikki had an older sister and a very loving family.

Nikki liked to spend time with her grandparents. Her grandfather loved to look at the stars in the night sky. He used to tell Nikki and her sister stories about the different groups of stars. He would also tell them tales of the heroes of ancient Greece and Rome.

Nikki loved to listen to her grandparents just talk to each other. They talked about everyday things—their town, people they knew, and the world they lived in.

Maybe this is where Nikki got her love of words and a love of the simple things in the world that she would later write about in her poems.

As a child, Nikki sometimes found it hard to make friends. She always felt that she was different from other children.

Even though she felt different, Nikki learned that she could use words to express herself. Later, she put those words into poems.

While Nikki was in college, she began to write about what life was like for African Americans in the United States. She knew what it was like to be treated badly just because of the color of her skin.

Nikki's first book of poems was published in 1968. It was called *Black Feeling, Black Talk*. She soon became one of the most famous African American writers in America. People everywhere began to read and respect her poetry.

After her son was born in 1969, Nikki began to think a lot more about what life is like for children. She found that she enjoyed writing about being a parent. Having a young son also helped her remember what it was like to be a child and to write poems about it.

During this time, Nikki wrote many poems for children. These poems paint pictures of what children are like and the things they do. Two of her books became very popular with both adults and children. They were called *Spin a Soft Black Song* and *Vacation Time: Poems for Children.*

Nikki uses things she remembers from her childhood in her poems. Some of these poems talk about the wonders of chocolate, oatmeal on winter mornings, sparkling stars, and dreams of riding rainbows.

Nikki also talks about how important it was for her to listen to her family's stories when she was young. She especially loved the sound of her family's voices and words. She says, "I want my writing to sound like I talk."

Today, Nikki still writes poetry. In her poems, she likes to point out things that other people might not notice or things they might not think are important.

Nikki also helps other poets to write poems. She believes that many different kinds of poems should be read. Because of Nikki, many new writers have had their poems published.

Growing up in a family of storytellers helped Nikki find her own voice. She says, "I'm lucky that I had the sense to listen and the heart to care. I'm glad they talked into the night, sitting in the glider on the front porch, Grandmother munching on fried fish and Grandpapa eating something sweet."

We are glad too that Nikki was a good listener. Otherwise, we might not have had the chance to read her wonderful poems.